The Left Behind

Some echoes never fade

Garrett Vargas

Copyright © 2026 by Garrett Vargas

This is a work of fiction. Names, characters, places, and incidents are either the product of the author's imagination or used fictitiously. Any resemblance to actual persons, living or dead, events, or locales is entirely coincidental.

All rights reserved. No part of this book may be reproduced, stored in a retrieval system, or transmitted in any form or by any means — electronic, mechanical, photocopying, recording, or otherwise — without the prior written permission of the author, except in the case of brief quotations embodied in critical articles or reviews.

Chapter ornaments sourced from Vecteezy, used under Free License with attribution

First paperback edition: January 2026
ISBN: 9798242760929

Contents

Chapter 1 1

Chapter 2 10

Chapter 3 17

Chapter 4 27

Chapter 5 42

Chapter 6 55

Chapter 7 66

Chapter 8 73

Chapter 9 78

Chapter 10 87

Chapter 11 91

Chapter 12 97

For my wife,

whose love has been the steady echo throughout my life

Chapter 1

The alarm clock rang with a shrill sound. Meigan Wilder rolled over and smacked it with a heavy arm to reclaim the silence. The last quarter had been tough, and she had forgotten to turn it off now that it was spring break. She sank back into her pillow, ready to resume her slumber, when a thought hit her. Today was the day that her older cousin Jennifer was coming to visit. Meigan jumped out of bed and started to get dressed.

Meigan was in her senior year at Mitchell High School in Colorado Springs, part of the clique of girls the rest of the school wanted to emulate. But to her, Jennifer was the one worthy of admiration. *Wow*, she thought, *it's great that our spring breaks lined up this year.* Jennifer had just landed a full-time job as a project manager for a prominent technology company and was in her final quarter of college. Meigan looked at the picture of the two of them taken together last year – they almost looked like twins.

She stared fondly at the photo as she admired the resemblance. At the same time, she resented her for presenting an image that Meigan felt compelled to emulate. She had gotten her nose pierced just like her cousin in February, much to the chagrin of her father. "Don't try to be someone you're not," she heard him boom, scolding her for getting her nose pierced without his permission. "Whatever, Dad," she muttered under her breath. *At least it helped you forget the tattoo*, she thought, admiring the striking colors on the arm-length tattoo from winter break.

His words echoed as she started to dress slowly, choosing each piece as someone chooses armor. The cut-off shorts and ribbed cotton top were great choices for blending in with the other girls. It didn't feel like her, not really, but it was the version of herself that belonged with the popular girls. She spent several minutes teasing her long, flowing hair, not out of vanity, but because it was what others expected to see. Then, on the nightstand, she picked up the four silver bracelets she had bought at a garage sale last summer; the only part of her outfit that was truly something she wanted to wear. She loved the way they clinked together. Sometimes, when she was feeling especially insecure, she would purposely swing her arm to hear the clinking noise they made. She slipped them on and let them land against each other admiring the sound.

A black BMV coupe pulled up to the curb. Jennifer stepped out of the driver's seat. She didn't walk towards the house as much as saunter with an air of sophistication and bravado that let everyone know she was ready to conquer the world. "You've grown up so much," she said as she eyed Meigan in the front doorway. "Are you ready to go?"

Meigan grabbed her jacket and hesitated. There was a part of her that wanted to stay home and avoid the performance she slipped into around her cousin. "Alright," she said, her fingers tightening around her worn leather jacket, "let's go."

By the time they reached a row of small local shops, the wind was starting to pick up. Meigan saw Pikes Peak in the distance, its snow-streaked ridge cutting the horizon with a calming presence. They entered Pete's Wild West Store, one of those kitschy old-timey stores where the inventory was stacked on top of itself. Underneath a misplaced cowboy hat and a pile of second-hand leather belts Meigan saw a silver-plated belt buckle. The buckle glinted in the fluorescent lighting as Meigan tried it on and found it to be a perfect size for her frame. "Wow, you look right out of the 1800s with that!" Jennifer exclaimed. "You should take it." Meigan took the buckle off and turned it over in her hands. "Made in China," it said on the back. *Yeah, authentic 19th century there*, she thought.

"Jennifer, this is $40. I don't have that kind of money," Meigan protested.

Jennifer looked slowly around before leaning in, her voice dropping to a whisper, and her tone just sharp enough to cut. "Just take it," she mouthed. Meigan held the buckle in her hands, its shine suddenly heavy. She knew it was wrong. She wanted to tell Jennifer no. The word rose in her throat, before she swallowed it back down as her cousin watched with that familiar, assessing look. Jennifer's approval was a weakness she couldn't shake. She deftly slipped the buckle into her jacket pocket, and the shame arrived before the metal even touched the leather. Meigan wanted to leave the store as quickly as possible. Each step towards the door knocked the metal against her side, a quiet reminder of the line she'd crossed.

"You did great," Jennifer said when they were outside. "Put it on. I want to see it in the light."

Meigan wanted to get as far away as possible but did as she was told while her stomach continued turning in knots. She was lost in introspection when someone tapped her on the shoulder. Frightened, she turned.

"Hi," a slightly older man said, holding a camera at his chest. Meigan thought it was an undercover cop, ready to take her mugshot. She winced. "I'm writing a piece for the Gazette about old western trends." She untensed her fists on hearing this. "I'd love to get a picture of you with that belt buckle. You look great in it!"

Racked with guilt, Meigan just wanted to leave. She turned to Jennifer who was smiling and eagerly nodding her head with approval. Meigan stood tall, put her fists to her side and said, "Sounds great, how's this look?" The pose was bold and photogenic, but it reflected nothing of what she felt inside, much like her wardrobe.

"Thanks," the reporter said. "Look for the article in tomorrow's paper!"

⁂

The following day was slightly less breezy, and a sunbeam peaked through the window as Meigan sat alone at Loyal Coffee, still wearing the buckle across her cut-off denim shorts and nursing a latte. She was anxiously jingling her silver bracelets, trying to stay grounded and to soothe the knots in her stomach that a frothed hot beverage just couldn't alleviate. Jennifer was back at the house taking a call about her upcoming job, and Meigan decided to take some alone time to try to reconnect with herself.

Wow they really got my good side, she thought as she looked at her picture in the newspaper on the table in front of her. She shifted the buckle in her lap as she admitted to herself that it looked good on her. But she couldn't shake the shame she felt from stealing it and the guilt from having it on display for everyone to see.

"Hey." She looked up. A boy her age stood beside her table, sporting a light jacket featuring a scattering of faded stars stitched in silver thread. The stars formed the constellations Cassiopeia on the left side, with Andromeda on the right. He was slinging a backpack over his shoulder as he greeted her, the blue nylon strap covering half of one of the constellations.

Nodding towards the paper on the table he said, "That's you in the Gazette, right?"

Meigan's stomach tightened. "Uh … yeah."

The boy smiled, not teasing, not mocking, just warm. "It's a good picture." Meigan blinked, caught a bit off guard and a little flattered that someone else liked the picture too. She started to fidget with her bracelets as she took in the praise. "Confident pose. But …," he paused for a moment, "you'd do well to internalize it."

Her face went hot. What did he mean by that? She shifted uncomfortably in her seat before stammering "I … I don't know what that means."

The boy shrugged. "Just an observation," he said as he finished putting the backpack over his shoulders. "Hope to see you around again," he added as he headed out, leaving her alone to ponder his words.

Meigan stared at the door after he left for a long moment. She looked down at the buckle as it sat in her lap, noticing her reflection in the over-shined finish. It was uncanny how he had verbalized just what she had been thinking. She finished her latte and left, leaving the paper behind. She started to walk back home, slowly and methodically. The crisp spring air whirled through her hair as the noise of the street competed with her thoughts. The Route 5 bus pulled up across the street and the people lined up at the stop started to board.

Someone shouted behind her. The sharp, urgent sound was swallowed by traffic, and Meigan turned her head just enough for her eyes to flick toward the noise. No one seemed to be looking at her. She shrugged it off and kept walking. She felt a faint hum press against her ears like the world inhaling ... and vanished.

The bus finished loading its passengers and pulled away.

Chapter 2

Her next step landed not on the concrete sidewalk but on soft ground, kicking up dirt as her heel made contact with the earth. Meigan flinched. The city sounds were gone. The air smelled like dust and horses, not smog. She stopped mid-stride and looked around. The bus had disappeared. The road had disappeared. The shopping mall, banks, and high rises were all … gone! Instead, Meigan found herself on a dirt road, winding lazily ahead of her towards a small collection of quaint wooden buildings with signs that swung gently in the wind sporting simple descriptions like "barbershop" or "saloon".

Her instinct was to stop dead in her tracks. Was Jennifer playing a trick on her? She turned around to see if Jennifer or another familiar face was watching her, but all she saw was some light dust and a tumbleweed in the distance kicking through the wind. A blank look crossed her face as she stood rooted, unsure what to do next.

After a moment, an instinct kicked in to walk forward. She progressed, slowly and timidly at first, unsure if the ground was going to give out beneath her. But as she approached the buildings and signs of other people, she hastened her stride, swaying her arms confidently to hear the soothing sound of the bracelets that gave her connection to reality. She could feel the buckle around her waist as she strode towards the crowd.

As she drew nearer, she heard a scream. A woman had spotted her and was pointing, mouth wide open. Meigan stopped for a moment, not as much from the screaming as from the appearance of the woman. The woman was wearing a long, beige cotton dress with full sleeves that looked like it had been stitched together at home. Her hem extended down to her scuffed boots, just high enough off the ground that they stayed out of the dirt but full enough to avoid any sense of impropriety. A tightly drawn bonnet on her head protected her from the sun, a job her clothing certainly wasn't doing. Meigan approached the lady to introduce herself, but the woman ran off in the other direction.

Odd woman, Meigan thought to herself. As she continued walking, she could sense people staring at her from the doorways of the plain buildings. Near the bank, a group of men wearing bowler hats and sporting suspenders stopped their conversation cold and had turned to gaze at her. A group of more women wearing similar homespun dresses were leaving the general store, their heads lowered and their hands raised to their faces to avoid more than brief glimpses of her as they crossed her path. She felt on display, almost violated, as she realized that she was the odd one out. The weight of their stares made her suddenly self-conscious of her bare legs, the metal rings around her wrists, the metal in her nose, and the ink on her skin. She hastened her pace, not towards anything in particular, but away from the eyes that tracked her.

At the end of the road, she saw two men arguing loudly with each other. The man doing most of the arguing was a younger man standing six feet tall. His rugged looks and dirt-worn trousers held up by thick, tan suspenders suggested he was someone who worked outside for a living. His short black hair just peeked out from under the wide-brim hat on his head that shook as he jerked his head in debate. The middle-aged man who was the target of the argument was wearing a tailored suit and carried a medical bag in his hand. He stood rigid and firmly rooted despite the passionate movements from the other man. He delivered his retorts with a firm but steady voice as he titled his chin up to return the younger man's fire.

As she approached, Meigan could overhear enough to make out that they were arguing over a bill and that the younger man was named Evan. Their voices were all twang and clipped-off words she'd only heard in old Westerns. They were so engaged in their own argument that they didn't notice her until she was standing right next to them.

"Hi," Meigan said. Her voice was hesitant and frail, but the words came out clearly. The men saw her and instinctively took a half step back before stopping to face her. "Can you tell me where to get the route 5?"

After some glances between themselves, Evan puffed up his chest, put his thumbs underneath his suspenders, and spoke. "Howdy, ma'am, the … route 5?" he said as he enunciated each word, "What in tarnish are you talking about?"

"The bus stop," Meigan said slowly letting each word land. "I seem to be lost."

"I don't know what y'er talking about," he said. Then eyeing her clothing and tattoo added, "ma'am I reckon you ain't well with that getup. Ma always says a girl shouldn't be out alone. My farm isn't far; she'll know how to get you properly dressed and get that thing out of your nose."

"No way," Meigan said firmly planting her hands to her waist in a defiant tone. "I'm not going anywhere with you."

Evan quietly flinched at this unexpected sign of defiance. He turned his head towards the doctor in confusion, looking for some advice. The doctor had one of his eyebrows cocked, and a half-formed snarl on his lips. Evan turned back towards Meigan and wagged his finger in her direction. "You need some proper clothes and a warm meal," he said calmly but firmly. "Pardon my directness but you ain't quite right."

Meigan still had a knot in her stomach and realized that it was perhaps partly caused by hunger. She knew better than to follow a strange man dressed like someone from the Old West back to his house alone. But as she had this thought, she remembered the past few moments ... everyone seemed dressed like these men in front of her. And the town itself ... did she see a saloon back there? Meigan spun around, finally taking in her surroundings. And she did something uncharacteristic of the confident woman she portrayed.

She fainted.

Chapter 3

Meigan awoke to the smell of woodsmoke wafting through the doorway. The room was dim, lit only by a single oil lamp on a rustic wooden table in one corner. She was lying on a thin, well-worn mattress with a heavy, handmade quilt pulled up to her chin. She slowly lifted her arm to her throbbing head and blinked her eyes. Slowly tilting her head, Meigan started to take in her surroundings. As the reality of the unfamiliar scene took root, she shot up in a state of panic, the quilt falling by her side.

"Easy there," she heard a voice say. Evan stood in the doorway, hat in hand, looking like he wasn't sure whether to step inside or flee. His voice was gentle but wary, as if he were addressing a skittish horse. "You took a spell," he said. "Dropped like a sack of feed."

Meigan looked down towards the floor, then turned towards him. While she had only recently met Evan, it was at least good to see a familiar face. "Yeah," she said as she rubbed the back of her head. "I must have fainted. Wow, I never pass out like that. Chemical imbalance."

Evan frowned. He furrowed his brow and slightly cocked his head, unsure of some of the words she had just uttered. He ultimately decided not to press but continued. "Yeah ... you hungry, ma'am? I've got stew on the stove. Rabbit and potatoes."

Rabbit? Had she heard him right? Meigan crinkled her face as thoughts of a bunny bouncing across the countryside crossed her mind. Shaking her head slightly, she continued to assess her surroundings, now noticing the things that weren't there. There was no TV, coffee maker, or even electric outlets. Perhaps rabbit stew wasn't that much of a stretch.

"Miss," the word cut through to her as she started to come out of her daze. "I don't reckon you're from any place I've heard tell of."

Meigan swallowed. No, she had to admit, these weren't familiar surroundings. She opened her mouth to respond when she suddenly got her first view out the window. There, looming in the background, was a familiar sight. The unmistakable snow-capped tops of Pikes Peak. "I ...," she stammered. She couldn't finish her sentence.

Evan was staring at her arm. The ink of the tattoo seemed to call to him. He had never seen one this close before, and certainly never on a woman. "That's some odd markin' you got," he said with a mix of concern and curiosity, pointing towards her arm, "someone put that on you?" Meigan drew back at this question, feeling accused, and placed her hand over the base of her tattoo. She was used to getting stares about her tattoo, but usually it was either from a sense of wonder or disapproval from a group she was trying to antagonize. But being called marked seemed extreme. As she drew back, she fumbled to pick up the quilt on the floor and covered herself up, bracelets jingling as they too ducked under cover, before the inevitable "shorts too high" line could land.

"'Sawright," Evan said noticing her discomfort and softening his tone. "Didn't mean to make you uncomfortable." As he said this, another figure appeared in the doorway. A stern-looking middle-aged man loomed. He was wearing overalls, dirty from an honest day's work but still falling neatly on his body. A modest, sensible hat with a wide brim topped his head, frayed at the edges from years of use. The air stood still as if the room itself knew this man deserved its respect. "Son," the man said bluntly. "Time for supper. Get her fed and ma and me will sort her out later."

On seeing his father, Evan straightened up and became colder again. "I'll go fetch you a bowl of stew. You need to eat somethin'," he told her. "Rest. And tomorrow we'll figure out how to make you less conspicuous." Meigan slowly nodded. "You mean hide me?" she softly asked.

"I mean keep you safe," Evan said, his voice gaining in composure as hers dropped in confidence. "This town ain't cruel but it ain't kind to what it don't understand." Having said that, he turned and followed his father out the door. Just before leaving, he quickly glanced back and tipped his hat in a small, awkward gesture of respect, leaving her to the dim lamplight and quiet creak of the old house settling around her.

⚜ ⚜

Meigan sat cross-legged on her mattress as she slowly picked at her stew on the floor beside her with crude, wooden utensils. It was a different taste, but satisfying nonetheless. Her mind was a mix of emotions; scared, confused, and angry all at the same time. Her thoughts bounced wildly from the conversation she just had, the sawdust at her feet, and how she might never see her parents or Jennifer again.

She scraped the bottom of her bowl reflexively as she stared mindlessly forward. The gamey taste of rabbit was quite filling. She pushed the bowl away and walked slowly towards the flickering lamp, her footsteps soft against the wooden floor. *Where am I?* she thought. As she stared out the window and caught another glance of Pikes Peak a realization slowly crossed her mind. *Or … when am I?*

As she was having these thoughts, two figures entered the doorway. Evan was standing, slightly hunched, with his hat in his hand. Next to him stood a woman who must have been in her late forties. She was erect, with a long homespun dress like the ones she had seen the women in town wearing. A faded off-white apron was tied across her waist. She stood five inches shorter than Evan but dominated the scene nonetheless. Meigan correctly inferred that this was Evan's mother.

"This the girl you told me 'bout?" the woman asked Evan while keeping her eyes fixated on Meigan. "Yes, ma," Evan said. "Saw her yesterday. Don't know where she come from."

Evan's mom scanned Meigan from top to bottom, taking in her clothes, her accessories, and her long flowing hair. She watched thoughtfully as Meigan shifted uncomfortably from her gaze then frowned and exclaimed in a stern voice, "Tarnation, girl! It ain't decent being out like that! Don't you have any shame?"

"Hey, you aren't my mother," Meigan said, trying to resist, though the words came out smaller than she had wanted and landed without any impact. "There's nothing wrong with my clothes."

"I never!" Evan's mom said her voice rising as she accented the last syllable. Meigan's resistance fell. "And what are those devil's markings?" Evan's mom continued pointing at her arm. "Something ain't right with you, woman. What are you doing walking around without a man?"

Meigan paused for a moment. She looked down as her shoes shuffled against the floor and confessed, "I'm here all alone. I don't know where my family or friends are."

Evan's mom stopped as she looked at the girl before her. She turned to look at Evan and could tell he sensed the same as her, that this wasn't a defiant devil's creature, but instead a scared, confused girl. Her tone softened as she walked closer to Meigan. "There, there," she said, as she patted Meigan's hand. "Look, you're scared, I can see that. We'll get you sorted. I'm Martha Whitaker. You met my son, Evan. This is our farm you're on. I see he fed you," she said, glancing towards the dishes. "I'll get you dressed proper." Martha turned to exit.

"Wait," Meigan said. She had a growing suspicion but wasn't sure how to ask the question. "What day is it?"

"Wednesday, April 21."

Wednesday? Wait, yesterday was the 20th, but it was a Monday. She was sure of it. At least, it was in 2015. She pressed on asking the question she wasn't sure she wanted to hear the answer to. "Umm … what year is it?"

"You gone forgetful?" Martha said, "It's the year of our lord eighteen hundred eighty." Meigan, who earlier would have fainted at this revelation, instead just slumped to the ground.

Martha, shaking her head and muttering to herself left with her son. A few minutes later, she returned to give Meigan her own simple, plain, and colorless garment. Meigan hated it.

"Put this on," Martha said in a tone that was both commanding and gentle, and Meigan did as she was told. "I made sure to get you one with the long sleeves, that'll cover up those marks. And take those ridiculous rings off your wrists."

My silver bracelets, Meigan thought. She hesitated. "No, not those. I…", her voice was weak and it wasn't even clear whether Martha heard her. "Now," Martha snapped as Meigan hesitated. The words died in Meigan's throat. She did as she was told. Martha stepped behind Meigan and, with the ease of years of practice, gathered her hair and tied it into a bun. "There, that should make you look a tad more respectable," she said as she stood back to admire her work.

The following day, Meigan stood on the porch of the main house. Her long modest dress left no hints of the tattoo underneath. Her hair was no longer flowing but instead sat neatly and conservatively tucked in a bun. There were no nasal jewelry, bold silver buckle, or bracelets that clinked. She was an attractive, well-dressed, and proper 1880s woman. She looked respectable but felt erased.

Chapter 4

It had been three weeks since Meigan arrived in 1880. She was starting to accept the possibility that she was going to be stuck in the past. It hadn't been an easy adjustment. It had taken her a week to get a good night's sleep on the worn-out mattress she'd been given, and almost daily she'd stumped her gracious host family by asking them to "turn on the lights" or "drive into town." But those lapses were becoming less frequent now. Despite her quirks, the Whitaker family had started to bring her into the family fold. She was invited to the family table for meals and Martha had taken it upon herself to give her lessons on the basics of 19th century etiquette. "A proper education for a lady," as she put it.

One afternoon, Meigan and Evan were walking into town to barter some eggs. She found it odd that Martha insisted Evan accompany her into town. She was perfectly capable of carrying eggs herself and fancied herself a good negotiator. *Better than Evan*, she told herself privately but had the sense to keep this opinion to herself. Evan was strutting a little slowly through the street. Meigan wanted to walk past him, to hurry on with their chore, but she remembered that a proper frontier woman always walked behind the man.

As they passed the bank, a young man stepped outside and approached Evan. "Evan," he called from across the road as he strode towards him. "Why, I haven't seen you in o'er a month. Is this that young lass what appeared in town a few weeks ago?" He looked at her, softly giggling nervously as if he were trying to justify his presence. "I heard she was something else."

"Jebediah," Evan said warmly, extending his arm to give the man a hearty handshake. "Yep, she just showed up 'bout three weeks ago out of nowhere."

"Hi, I'm Meigan," Meigan said extending her arm as Evan had. Jebediah looked at her oddly, and Meigan quickly drew her arm back, realizing that she was interrupting men talking. *A woman should only speak when spoken to*, she heard Martha's voice echo in her head. The daily lessons seemed antiquated, but she was doing her best to internalize them to fit in.

"Well, she's certainly a fiery one," Jebediah said with a nervous laugh. The men continued their conversation exchanging pleasantries for a few more moments before Jebediah finally addressed her directly, tipping his hat as he did so. "Ma'am, been good to make your acquaintance." Meigan smiled back. "Best be on my way, give my regards to your ma."

The following afternoon, Martha was alone preparing for dinner. Rabbit stew had become one of Meigan's favorite dishes, and Mr. Whitaker had just shot a wild rabbit that morning. The men were out tending to the farm when there was a knock at the door. "Why Jebediah, good to see you," Martha said on answering the door. "Haven't seen hide of you in months. What brings you by?"

"Well, Mrs. Whitaker," Jebediah said with his hat in his hand and an even more nervous tone than the day before. "I come to ask you about that young lady Meigan you got staying here. I'd be interested in courtin' her if she is available."

Martha was pleased with herself for the transformation she'd been able to achieve but successfully hid the emotion from showing on her face. Despite some subtle prodding, she hadn't been able to coax Evan into courtin' her himself. She sure wished he'd settle down; the town was starting to talk about a 23-year-old man still living with his parents. Still, if she could marry off Meigan it would be a huge validation of her efforts. "Let me think it over and you come back tomorrow, OK?" she said dryly to Jebediah. She wanted to try one last time with her own son before approving.

This rabbit was larger than the last one, and Martha thought it would be too big for them to finish that evening. She had underestimated the appetites of her husband, Evan, and Meigan. "Let me clear the dishes, Mrs. Whitaker," Meigan said respectfully once Mr. Whitaker had finished licking his spoon clean. Martha nodded with a smile as Meigan gathered the plates and took them into the kitchen. After she was out of earshot, Martha leaned back in her chair and turned to her son. "Your friend Jebediah come by this afternoon," she said as she folded her arms neatly in her lap. "Wants to go a'courting with Meigan." She studied the look on Evan's face as she said this.

Evan's jaw tightened for a moment, then relaxed. "Well, if you ask me," he said in a deliberate, thoughtful voice, "she's still too disoriented to be courtin' yet. But suppose she should be looking for a man soon enough." Evan tapped his fingers slowly on the table. "You know best."

Martha flicked her eyes towards Evan with a hint of something unreadable. She could tell he wasn't thinking about Meigan in that way for himself, at least not yet. His father was not quite as subtle, as he dropped his fist to the table. "Speaking of courtin'," he said a little too loudly, "when are you going to look to settle down?" Evan tugged at his collar uncomfortably, while Martha gave her husband a stare.

"We'll tell Jebediah he can court Meigan," she said ignoring her husband's question and putting an end to the conversation as she saw Meigan returning. "He would be a nice match for her." Martha perked back up in her chair and addressed Meigan directly, "Meigan, do you remember meeting Jebediah the other day?"

"Sure," she said. "Seemed like a nice fella." She was learning how to pepper in some of the dialect from the times in her speech.

"Well, he's interested in courtin' you. I think it'd be a fine match."

Meigan recoiled. She was still adjusting to this era and still had a flicker of hope that she'd be able to return to her own time, though admittedly the possibility seemed to fade with each passing day. She wasn't too keen on settling down here. "Courting? You mean, dating? Oh no, Mrs. Whitaker, I'm not ready for that," Meigan started to protest.

Martha gave her a cold stare, "Well I think it's a fine idea and I'm gonna tell him yes. See how it goes. I'll go with you your first time out, make sure he's an honest gent for ya."

This was too much, Meigan protested, but Martha remained steadfast. Meigan had come to learn that she was no match for the older woman's stubbornness, and caved in. She told herself that at least it would be nice to get out and meet some new people. As she acquiesced, she sat back down in her chair, folding her hands neatly in her lap.

The courtship didn't last long. Despite outward appearances and behavioral shifts, Meigan still wasn't a fit in the time period, and it became apparent to Jebediah that she was "too weird" as he later told Martha. That was fine with Meigan. To her he seemed to want to rush into talking about relationships, when she just wanted to hang out and experience new people. "Well, we'll try again," Mr. Whitaker said. Though a bit disappointed it hadn't worked out, Martha was secretly happy, hoping that Evan would come around and finally get hitched himself.

❧ ☙

As early spring turned to late summer, Meigan's thoughts of her life in 2015 were becoming more infrequent. Sometimes she'd go days at a time not thinking about Jennifer, her dad, or the amenities she was missing in this new timeline. Martha had continued her daily lessons with Meigan to help her fit into her new surroundings. Those efforts were paying off, as she was starting to establish social relationships with other young women that didn't involve pointing or gawking.

Even though Meigan was adopting well, she still felt out of touch. While she appreciated that people were accepting her, she still felt a sense of emptiness inside. She was fitting in but not really herself.

One afternoon while out in town, she saw three of her friends gathered around each other in conversation. They were leaning in, speaking in whispered tones as they usually did. Despite usually not having anything to say that required discretion, Meigan had realized that this was the way they interacted and had started to adopt. As she approached, they made space for her to join their circle. One of them addressed her not with a pleasantry but with a question, "you hear about the Walton family?"

The Waltons were a family that lived about a quarter mile from the Whitaker farm. Meigan knew them well enough; a young husband and wife with a happy two-year old son. They had moved into Colorado Springs two months before Meigan had arrived, though their journey had been met with much less controversy than hers. They had set up their home in the valley at the base of one of the hills. "Lord be," another woman said as Meigan shook her head to indicate she hadn't heard the latest gossip about them, "I heard they been getting sick. Doc don't know what could be causin' their sickness. Thinks it's some bad humors."

Meigan was genuinely moved by this news. This wasn't idle gossip, this could be something serious. She gasped and put her hand slightly over her chest. "No!" she said. "Yep, sure are," the first woman responded. "And they been sick this past two weeks. Not sure what they gonna do to help."

"Didn't they build their outhouse up on the hill?" Meigan asked, reflectively. She was recalling something from her science class the previous quarter. Something about this seemed familiar.

"Sure, but don't know what that got to do with things. They ain't weak enough they can't still get up the hill."

"Don't you see," Meigan said as the pieces fell into place in her head, "the waste is seeping down and contaminating the well! They shouldn't be drinking the water from it." She raised her voice as she said this, rapidly expressing her concern. The weight of the situation overcame her attempts to fit in.

"What you be saying?" one of the women said, eyeing her. "You think the water be what causin' this?"

"Yes," she said urgently. "We best let doc know."

As luck would have it, the doctor was just stepping out of the barber shop. The women looked his way, unsure what to do. Meigan didn't hesitate and walked right up to him. The other women looked at each other, shocked at her boldness. One of them broke from the group and followed several steps behind her.

Meigan called out to the doctor to get his attention. "Mornin', Miss Wilder," the doctor said turning around and tipping his hat. Meigan explained her theory. The doctor puzzled over it, not sure about it, but nodded, "well, can't hurt none to have them try drinking from a different well."

Within three weeks, the family had healed, and word spread of her quick thinking and confidence in addressing a man of medicine so directly. The chatter didn't focus on the scandal, but rather theorized that without her the Walton family may not have been saved. Mr. Whitaker had even commented, "that was some quick thinking," which was about the highest compliment you could expect from him.

❧ ☙

One fall evening, Meigan was helping dust the furniture in Martha's room when she saw her silver bracelets and buckle in a box by the window. It briefly took her back to her former life. With a swallow she summoned the courage to ask, "Mrs. Whitaker, I was wondering. You think I could wear my silver bracelets? I always liked the way they felt."

Far from being upset, Martha was supportive of this request. "Well shoot, girl, those bracelets would look nice with your dress. Give you a bit of a unique look. The buckle too, I think that'd be a mighty fine look."

Meigan was visibly excited by this suggestion. She did love the buckle, but she also remembered that she had stolen it from Pete's Western Wear shop before being transported back here. The smile slowly disappeared from her face. "No, ma'am, I don't think I'd take the buckle. Don't feel I deserve it."

"Why not, silly child?" Martha said, "it'd look nice on you."

Meigan lowered her head, then slowly confessed, "I got somethin' I oughta tell you. I stole that belt buckle."

"Why child," Martha said gently, with a small, stifled laugh, "that must've been ages ago! I admire your honesty though and I see you know you did wrong. Tell ya what, iff'n you want to do some extra chores round the farm we'll say you earned that buckle fair and square. Why don't you start tending to the chickens before you help me make breakfast in the morning?"

"Really?" Meigan said, excited. "You got a deal, Mrs. Whitaker!" She slipped the bracelets on her arms, hearing them clink against each other, a sound she hadn't heard in months. She practically skipped out of Martha's room. On her way back to her room, she saw Evan sitting at the table, whittling on a stick. Upon hearing the clicking of the bracelets, he looked up and smiled at her.

"Those look right nice on you," he said. "I remember first time I saw you with those. But look at you now, they're a good fit." She stopped, flattered. Then, pulling up a chair to the table, she sat down on the other side of him.

"Thanks Evan, they do feel right now," she said, slowly twisting her bracelets. "You know, I see you when you're around pa," Evan froze and stopped mid-stroke on his work. "I know what it's like to feel like you have to be someone else. You don't have to be like him. You're a good man just the way you are." Evan was at a loss for words. He took a last glance at her before looking down and continuing to whittle. He inhaled sharply before responding, "'Suppose so. Good night, Miss Meigan." She decided to leave the conversation at that. She pushed out her chair, rose, and with a brief "good night," left Evan with his whittling and his thoughts.

Chapter 5

A month later, the first signs of winter were rolling into town. A hush had fallen over the land as the air cooled and the wind blew the scent of snow from the mountains. This was the type of weather Meigan loved best; the cold winter kiss on her face while still being able to walk without being knee deep in snow. She was wearing her hard-earned buckle, letting it shine in the setting sun as her silver bracelets slowly clinked against each other. She still sported her tattoo, but as always it was invisible underneath her sleeves. As she passed neighboring farms, she glanced and smiled at the men busy stacking wood for the upcoming season.

Approaching the Charleston farmhouse, she saw large puffs of dark smoke coming from the chimney. Crinkling her nose as an acrid smell filled her lungs, she altered her path to walk up to their front door. When she knocked, Mr. Charleston opened the door a bit short of breath. "Afternoon, Miss Meigan," he panted. "Pardon my rudeness, but I ain't got time for socializin' just now, we got a bit of a chimney fire I'm tryin' to put out."

"Goodness!" she exclaimed. "Is there anything I can do to help?"

"No, don't worry yourself miss," Mr. Charleston said as his wife rushed by behind him with a bucket swaying clumsily. "We just got some buckets of water and we're gonna put it out."

Meigan tilted her head. This wasn't the right way to put out a fire. How did that saying go? *Starve the flame, shut the frame.* "Water's not going to help with that," Meigan said abruptly recalling her childhood lesson. "What you need is to starve the flame. Close the flue, that'll put it out."

Mrs. Charleston, in earshot of this advice, stopped before she had reached the fire. She looked at her husband, not sure what to do. Mr. Charleston turned his head and looked at her with eyes that showed he too was confused before turning again to face Meigan. He hesitated, clearly unsure, but something in her tone convinced him. He turned back to his wife and nodded. She closed the flue and within minutes the flames had been extinguished.

"Well, I'll be," Mr. Charleston said to Meigan. "How'd you know that?"

Meigan, resuming a modest demeanor, simply shrugged her shoulders and said, "just a hunch."

The following night, Meigan stood in her room, capturing a glimpse of herself in the mirror. Word was spreading about her new look. But by now, she wasn't being gawked at or shunned for the bracelets she wore, or the buckle she sported. She stopped, stood erect and admired her look. She was feeling something different. She wasn't just fitting in; she was an individual.

Evan passed by unnoticed as she was admiring her reflection. He saw her out of the corner of his eye at first, then stopped and took a step backward to fully absorb the scene. He lingered for just a moment, not long enough to be detected, but long enough to appreciate the transformation in her and some deeper feelings within himself.

❧ ☙

A few days later, Meigan was sitting at the breakfast table, reading about the latest silver find in Leadville. Martha had spared her the usual breakfast cleanup chores, letting her quietly read the paper after the men had left for the fields. As Meigan gently licked her finger to turn the page of the paper there was a knock on the door. Martha answered to find a fifteen-year-old girl with blonde braided hair and a bulky jacket to protect her from the cold. She was holding a loaf of bread ceremoniously with both hands, as if dropping it would shatter it.

"Why Emma," Martha said as she welcomed the Charleston family's eldest daughter inside, "it's so nice to see you. Heard you had a bit of a fright the other day."

"Yes'm," Emma said with a slight curtsy. "That's why I'm here. The folks wanted to thank Miss Meigan for helpin' us with her quick thinkin'."

"Well, she's right over there," Martha said, as she pointed to Meigan and returned to cleaning up. Emma approached, lowered the bread onto the center of the table and addressed her. "My family's deeply grateful you come by when you did. You saved us all."

"Oh, weren't nothing," Meigan said humbly. Emma leaned over Meigan's shoulder and peered at the paper. "What'cha doing there?" she asked Meigan confused. "I don't see no pictures."

Meigan noticed the confused look in Emma's eyes as she gazed at the paper, tilting her head and furrowing her brow. "Emma," she asked with her own hint of confusion, "what's the matter? Can't you read?"

"'Course not," Emma said as if the question itself were silly. "Pa never taught me letterin'. Don't know any girls who know readin'."

Meigan was surprised, but as Emma said this, she thought back to the mornings when Martha would scoop up the paper after Evan and Mr. Whitaker were done without reading it herself. Come to think of it, she couldn't recall any time she'd seen any of the women reading. In fact, on the rare occasions that she herself was able to read the paper, Martha always seemed to make sure it was while the men were away.

Meigan sat for a long, uncomfortable while as she thought about the expectations of women at the time against the tragedy of a generation of women unable to read. Something in her stirred and she whispered to Emma, low enough that Martha couldn't hear, "Emma, how'd you like to learn to read and write like me?"

Emma's eyes widened with a sense of both wonderment and fear. "Is that allowed?" she gasped, whipping her head to ensure Martha wasn't looking at them before continuing in a hushed voice. "I'd love to, but I don't think Pa will approve." Meigan nodded softly, a gesture that showed she both understood and disapproved. "Come by in the afternoon after your chores," she said. "Before your Pa comes home. It can be our secret."

That winter, Emma began slipping into the house each afternoon after her chores, her cheeks red from the cold winter air, and her eyes bright with the thrill of the lesson to come. The two of them would sit, books and papers strewn across the kitchen table, while Martha periodically checked out the window to alert them if anyone else approached.

At the same time, another development was happening in the Whitaker household. Evan had mustered up the resolve to start courting Meigan. Unlike Jebediah though, Evan found Meigan's unique style and growing sense of independence charming, not weird. In fact, when she confessed to him what she was doing with Emma, he didn't even flinch. "That's might nice," he said supportingly. "But we best not let pa know," he added with a chuckle.

One afternoon during their normal instruction, Martha glanced out the window and called out,

"Emma, your father is headin' this way." Emma and Meigan quickly gathered their papers and tucked them off to the side. There was a loud series of knocks on the door, and Meigan answered.

"Mr. Charleston," she said with a small smile, "it's great to see you. Please, come inside."

"Thank you, Miss Meigan," he muttered as he entered. "I heard Emma's been comin' here to learn letterin," he then said angrily, half addressing Meigan and half glancing at his daughter who was slowly shrinking under the table. Meigan shifted her body to block the father's glare and stated in a neutral tone, "yes, she has. A girl's got as much a right to learn as anyone."

Mr. Charleston shifted uncomfortably and said, "Well I don't take well to her learnin', she's got her place in our family and people'll talk."

Meigan paused for a moment and leaned slightly back as he spoke. Gaining confidence and composure, she said simply, "Let them talk. She has the right."

"Right?" he retorted. "That ain't for you to decide, she's my daughter."

"I'm not taking her from you," Meigan calmly responded. "I'm giving her something she can use."

Mr. Charleston stopped, surprised by the pushback. As he stood speechless, he noticed that Evan had returned home and was standing by Meigan's side. He had been coming home early from his afternoon chores to linger near the kitchen as Meigan taught. "She's safe here," Evan said as Mr. Charleston looked anxiously at him. "And she's learnin' something honest."

Mr. Charleston took this in quietly. After a pause that lingered in the air a bit too long, he grunted and called out to Emma, "Come on Emma, let's go home." Emma rose and moved towards him, shoulders hunched. His eyes followed her as she left. As he passed the doorway he paused, and turning back towards Meigan he said, "I'll bring her by tomorrow afternoon. 'Suppose there ain't no harm her learning some."

Over the following year, Meigan continued to teach more young girls how to read and write. While she still tried to do it all in secrecy, as more girls came to the Whitaker house each afternoon it was only natural that more rumors started to surface about her makeshift school. Eventually Meigan stopped hiding what she was doing and simply opened the door to let the girls file in without apology.

The months stretched to years, and Meigan's memories of the world she'd left dissolved while this unfinished town grew familiar enough to feel like home. As the number of girls gathering in the kitchen started to interfere with Martha's ability to prepare supper, Evan started constructing a new building on the farm. His father reluctantly chipped in as the following winter threatened to stall the completion of the project. When the make-shift schoolhouse opened its doors on a snowy December afternoon, a dozen girls were dropped off by their mothers and even a few curious fathers who wanted to see the new classroom.

The following summer, the classroom served another purpose as it was used to shelter the guests gathered for Evan and Meigan's wedding reception when an unseasonal rain hit the farm. It was cramped with the number of townsfolk who had come to see the newlywed couple, but no one complained as they stood elbow to elbow during Martha's toast, leaning in to hear over the sound of the rain beating on the roof.

By 1886, Meigan had taught scores of young girls how to read and write, but she wanted to take her efforts further. Reading and writing were important skills for young girls to learn, but she lamented that the young teenagers in her class had no proper education beyond her tutoring.

One evening, as Meigan and Martha were waiting for their stew to finish simmering, Evan came home with a young woman dressed in a crisp white blouse and long, brown pleated skirt that reached down to her ankles. A dark, black bowtie at her neck completed the woman's professional wardrobe.

"Ma, Meigan, I'd like to introduce you to Miss Sumner," Evan said as the young woman entered the kitchen.

"Abagail," the woman said as she gave a small curtsy. "I'm pleased to make your acquaintance."

"Miss Sumner teaches over at the schoolhouse," Evan said. "Please miss, have a seat," he added as he pulled a chair back from the kitchen table and gestured for her to sit down.

"No, thank you," Abagail said, "I can see you're getting ready to eat soon and I won't be long. Mrs. Whitaker," she said addressing Meigan, "our town is growing and the city council has approved adding another building to our school. With the extra students expected to come, I've asked if we can add another teacher to help, which the council has graciously agreed to. I've heard quite a lot about the work you're doing here with the local girls, and I wanted to see if you'd like to help me and continue that work at our school."

Martha gasped slightly as she heard this, while Meigan politely crossed her arms at her waist and addressed Abagail, "Miss Sumner, that is a fine offer," she said. "but will the school and the council encourage more girls to stay on and get their educations? Too many of them come to my school because they don't feel they have other options."

Abagail titled backwards slightly and smiled. "Why of course," she said, "why do you think you were the first person I wanted to ask about this role?"

Meigan smiled slightly, enough to show her pleasure without being improper. "Abagail," she said, "I would be honored to join you."

Chapter 6

It was 1908. The air had been dry the past few days, and Meigan was in the kitchen preparing supper after returning from school. Evan had just come home, closing the door quickly behind him to prevent the wind from blowing in debris, and was spending time with their young daughter Sarah. Sarah, now six, had been born well into their marriage, an unconventional gap for the time, and the source of a minor scandal in the town, which the two of them brushed off as just town gossip.

Meigan had gotten out the ingredients for Sarah's favorite food, cheesy noodles, and was chopping vegetables for the rest of the supper when she looked up. "Evan," she asked in a slightly alarmed tone. "Do you smell smoke?"

Evan put down the doll that he and Sarah had been playing with to look out the window. "My god," he said, "it looks like there's smoke over at the Barnaby farm!"

Meigan was already untying her apron. "Sarah, you're going to have to wait for supper," she said as she rolled up her sleeves and headed for the door. Evan was right behind her grabbing his hat and boots. "Sarah," he said turning back as he left the house, "stay inside and keep the door latched. We'll be back as soon as we can."

At the barn, Meigan joined a crowd that had gathered to watch the fire. The women were in the background, talking and swooning at the scene while the men, along with Meigan, were huddled talking about what to do. "Send some more men to fill up buckets from the well," one of them ordered. "Sure thing, Jeb," Evan responded. "Come on, let's go," he quickly directed two other men in the circle. "There's a well near town square. We can get there and back in ten minutes." So ordering, he grabbed three buckets, put them into the hands of the others, and they disappeared without another word.

"How are the Barnabys doing?" Meigan asked, looking around for signs of the family. "They seem to be safe, over there," Jeb mentioned, casually pointing towards the field. Meigan followed where he was pointing and headed to the family, alone in the field.

"Barb, Eliah, I see Susie here ... but where's Johnny?" she asked, frantically looking around.

Eliah, weak from the fumes, could barely speak. "He's ... he's still inside," he coughed, trembling from the smoke. Barb sat coughing and weeping as he said this, "He's in the loft. We weren't able to get him out!"

Meigan rose and turned her attention to the barn, still ablaze. She ran towards it without a second thought.

Meanwhile, a quarter mile away, a reporter dressed in fine tailored clothes leaned back in his chair. His dress suggested he wasn't from this humble town. He was putting a pad of paper filled with scribbled notes into a briefcase. A tripod leaned against the large desk that sat between him and a mustached man sitting on the other side. The reporter stood, reached awkwardly across and shook the other man's hand. "Thank you for your time, Mr. Secretary," he said, "this will make a fine article about your town."

"No, thank you, Mr. Dillon," the secretary of the chamber of commerce responded. "And ... what in blazes is that?"

The well sat just in view of the window of the secretary's office and he had caught glimpse of three men running towards it. The first man had dropped the bucket into the well while the others pulled on the rope to lift it as fast as they could. The secretary stood from this chair, while Francis Dillon, with the keen sixth sense that made a good reporter, quickly excused himself. By the time he reached the well, the first man had already run off, and the rope was being yanked up to fill the second bucket.

"There's a fire at the Barnaby farm!" one of the men yelled as Francis approached, his attention more focused on filling his bucket than on the reporter. "Come on, help us put it out!"

Francis, not a natural fire fighter, grabbed his briefcase and camera and followed. The man raced ahead with the urgency needed to help avert disaster, but Francis was still able to track him across the plains to find the farm. *Tragedy sells*, he thought to himself as he stepped through the hay fields, ignoring the mud sticking to his shoes. *This will make this fluff piece even better.*

Arriving at the scene, Francis looked around. This was, sadly, an all too familiar sight for him. A barn burning, a family huddled on the field, the men in action trying to put the fire out, while the women sat around in the background. But then ... he saw something different.

Meigan emerged from the barn, carrying little Johnny over her shoulder. Francis watched in amazement as she brought the boy to the family and then turned to the men to see how she could help more. She grabbed a bucket of water and raced back to the barn to help extinguish the flames. *This would be an amazing story*, he thought. *A woman saving a boy from a burning farm. My editor will love it!*

After the fire was safely put out and the townsfolk were in a slightly calmer state, Francis approached Meigan. "Pardon me ma'am," he said holding his hat in one hand and tripod in the other. "Mind posing for a photo for the paper?"

Meigan was still a bit bewildered. "Sure," she said, slightly distracted. "If you think it'll help."

Meigan stood with the remains of the barn in the background and Johnny at her side. She had rolled her sleeves partway up to counter the heat of the flames, exposing the bottom half of her tattooed arm, covered in soot. The silver bracelets she always wore sat at the end of her wrist, tarnished but still clinking. Her belt buckle reflected the dying embers from the extinguished fire.

"Thank you, ma'am," Francis said packing up his equipment. "This will be a great story!"

❧ 6 ☙

Evan and Meigan got home late that evening, clothes still smelling of smoke, boots heavy with ash. Before either could speak, a small voice cried from the front room. "Mom? Dad? When's supper?"

Meigan winced. In all the chaos, she had forgotten entirely about Sarah. Evan saw the guilt flash across her face. "You go to bed," he said gently. "You had a long evening. I got this." Meigan nodded, exhausted, and slipped into the bedroom to wash up and rest. Meanwhile, Evan stooped down and called Sarah towards him. She gleefully put down her doll and ran to her father's side.

"Sorry we weren't able to make you somethin' proper tonight," Evan said. "How about some beans and the last of the morning porridge?" Sarah, happier to see her father than picky about her food choices, simply said, "Yum!"

"You know," Evan said as he rose and started rummaging through the cupboard to find some beans. "Your ma won't want to say nothin', but she's a bit of hero. You know that kid Johnny Barnaby from school?"

Sarah nodded vigorously.

"Well, their barn caught fire. Bad one. Johnny was still inside," Evan said, choosing his words carefully. "Your ma went in after him. Pulled him out before the roof came down."

"Didn't anyone else see?" Sarah asked, mouth wide open.

"Nope, your mom's real perceptive like that," Evan said as he poured the beans into a pot. "She had some sense something weren't right and she wasn't going to let someone suffer. There was a reporter there from the Post up in Denver," he added. "Took her picture. Said he'd write it up."

"Can I see it, Dad? When's it comin' out?"

Evan smiled. "I'll fetch the paper tomorrow. But don't go fussin' over your ma about it. She ain't one for glory."

"I won't," Sarah promised.

Evan returned from the fields the next afternoon with a folded newspaper tucked under his arm. Sarah met him at the door.

"Did they print it?"

He handed her the paper. There, on the front page, was Meigan. Soot-streaked, eyes fierce and determined. Strands of her hair, normally held tightly in place, shot out as testaments to her heroism.

"They made her look real nice," Sarah whispered.

Evan nodded, "They surely did."

Word spread fast. By the next morning, Meigan couldn't walk Sarah to school without being stopped multiple times by neighbors and shopkeepers. "Meigan, you're a hero," Abagail said as Meigan dropped Sarah off with her before going to her own classroom. "We're going to have to have you come in and tell the younger students about it!"

"Oh, 'twas nothing," Meigan murmured, cheeks pink. "Just did what needed doing." But the attention made her uneasy. She hadn't saved Johnny for praise. She had done it because she couldn't bear the thought of losing a child.

After a week, the excitement faded. The town returned to its routines. Life settled back into its familiar rhythm. But soon, far too soon, it shifted again.

Sarah was still a child, just eleven years old, when her mother fell ill. It started small; a sharp stomach pain Meigan brushed off as something she'd eaten. "I can shake this," she said, as she leaned on the countertop to help navigate the kitchen. By morning she was pale and sweating, doubled over, and unable to stand. Evan sent for the doctor, but there was little he could do. "Her appendix has burst," he said quietly, hat in hand. "If we had caught it sooner … or if we had the means…"

Sarah remembered the way her mother tried to smile at her through the pain, shielding her from the extent of her suffering. By morning she seemed to be recovering; she was still weak but was lucid. Evan let her rest against his shoulder as the two of them walked into the kitchen to sit at the table. Sarah smiled on seeing her mother up and gave her a big, warm hug which Meigan returned with a tear streaking down her cheek.

The three of them sat around the table playing a round of twenty questions. As usual, Sarah was winning, teasing her mom for only picking things from within the house. They played until Meigan's smile began to fade and she asked to return to bed. By nightfall, the fever had taken hold again. Evan sat by her bedside all night, holding her hand and whispering that everything would be alright. By dawn, Meigan was gone. Taken by something that, in another time, would have been simple to treat.

The town mourned a hero. Sarah mourned her mother. And the legend began.

Chapter 7

Birds chirped overhead in the crisp November air as a yellow taxicab slowly drove down a quiet road in a small suburban town. The car slowed as it passed each house, as if searching for the right location. Finally, coming to a stop, a young woman in her early 20s stepped out of the cab. She carefully removed a wad of bills from the pocket of her turquoise wool jacket. As the driver placed her large hardcase luggage on the curb, she peeled some bills off to settle the fare. She stood on the sidewalk for a moment watching the cab pull away before turning towards the house.

It was 1965, and Clara had returned to Colorado Springs to visit her parents. Thanksgiving was coming up, and Clara had made the long trek from Simmons College to visit for a week. It had taken almost 15 hours through a few connecting cities to get here from Boston. As she awkwardly lugged her suitcase onto the porch, she reflected that it was worth it to see her folks.

Clara hadn't even rung the doorbell when the door opened and a woman in her mid-60s gingerly approached, embracing her in a huge hug. A casual observer might mistake this for her grandmother, but it was her mother, Sarah, who like Meigan before her, had waited until later in life to settle down and have children.

"Clara," Sarah exclaimed. "I'm so happy to see you! Wow, you've matured into such a fine woman," she said as she eyed her daughter from head to toe. It had been a year and a half since Clara had been home, as she had spent her summer interning for the Library of Congress.

"It's great to see you too, mom," Clara said enthusiastically. "Is Dad around?" she added, looking anxiously through the open doorframe.

"No honey," Sarah said. "He's out picking up some of the things I need for Thanksgiving dinner. But that will give us a chance to sit and talk. Come, I want to show you something."

As Clara entered the house, she noticed a large, leather trunk in the middle of the living room, its brass fixtures giving it a weathered look from a forgotten time. The frail woman had obviously had help placing it there, though Clara wasn't sure what secrets this trunk contained.

"I thought maybe with that library science degree, you'd be interested in going through some of these papers with me," Sarah said.

Clara smiled and stood a few inches taller. "Well, I don't have the degree just yet, mom," she corrected. "Still have another semester to go." She watched as Sarah gingerly bent down and opened the top of the trunk. "But I'm excited to see what you have here."

Clara peered into the trunk and saw a mismatched collection of photographs and random mementos including some tarnished silver bracelets and a belt buckle, both apparently untouched, perhaps out of remembrance. Her mother started rummaging through the top pile of papers before pulling out one of interest.

"These are keepsakes from our family," Sarah said, then with a slight tear in her eye, "mainly passed down from my dad about your grandma Meigan." She paused as she said this, with a hint of sad nostalgia crossing her face before composing herself to turn to Clara and smile. "I told you about the time she saved that boy from the fire, but I thought you might like to see this newspaper article about it."

Clara did indeed remember. The story of the fire had been burned into her psyche from years of retelling. Growing up, she wished she could have met her. She sounded truly ahead of her time.

Clara turned her attention away from her mother and the trunk between them and let her mind drift towards thoughts of her childhood. She remembered from a young age hearing about how Meigan had taught half the girls in town to read. When she was six, they had driven to the site of her grandparents' farm, by then abandoned, to see the crude wooden building that had served as the classroom. Tiles from the roof had fallen and lay scattered amidst some planks that the weather had torn off the sides over the years, but the structure was intact enough to allow them to walk inside. It was there that her mother gave her one of the books that Meigan had read with her when she was that age, a touching memento that had sparked Clara's own obsession with reading and lead her to library science.

Sarah sat at a distance, lovingly watching the reflective look on her daughter's face and unwilling to break the silence. Eventually, as Clara let out a knowing sigh and turned her eye back towards her mother, she continued. "I always loved this picture of her," Sarah said as she delicately handed the article to her daughter. Clara glanced at the headline, LOCAL HEROINE SAVES CHILD FROM FIRE, before her eyes landed on the picture. The woman looking back was worn and tired but still managed to strike a confident pose. Clara almost felt that Meigan was staring directly at her, as if daring her to make something of her life. *She had just saved that boy from certain death*, she thought. *And she still looks great*. She noticed the silver bracelets and belt buckle and realized they were the same items that she had seen earlier in the trunk. She wore them perfectly in that photo. She noticed the long sleeves of her dress rolled up, showing an arm half covered in soot.

Sarah could see Clara intently examining the photo. "You know, you're both pioneers in your own way," she said.

Clara brushed this comment off. *Me, a pioneer like Meigan?* she thought. *If only*. She then stopped for a moment, a quizzical look coming over her face. Turning to her mother and angling the photo towards her she asked, "Mom, doesn't her arm look more like it might be a tattoo?"

Sarah looked at the photo. She hadn't seen it for ten years, but when Clara said that she examined it again with fresh eyes. She had always thought it was just soot. After all, why would a woman in the early 20th century be sporting a tattoo.

"You know, you might be right," Sarah said nodding. "Very good eyes," she added.

Just then they heard a loud, popping engine outside. "Dad still hasn't gotten the car fixed, huh," Clara chuckled.

"No, he hasn't," Sarah laughed back. "I'd better go help him bring in the groceries. He'll be happy to see you."

"Me too," Clara said. "You have a lot of neat stuff in here," she said as she put the photo back into the trunk before standing to greet her father. "I'm going to go through this some more while you help dad."

Sarah smiled and nodded approvingly.

Chapter 8

Two figures stood on a familiar porch, but this time the door didn't swing open as they approached. They didn't bother to knock. Instead, the woman slipped out a key, turned the lock and the two slowly entered. A bit of dust kicked up from the unswept floor as they entered.

Clara didn't need this. Not now. She had spent eighteen years in the Denver Public Library's Western History Department, rising to Head Archivist for Special Collections. The role had once required her to lead a team of four people, but three months ago the whole department had been laid off as the library focused on "computerizing." How could they let her go after so many years of loyalty? They had offered to give a positive letter of recommendation, but computerizing wasn't just isolated to this department or this library. It was hard to find a role anywhere. Now amid that job search, her mother had passed away. She barely had the strength to make it here. Thank God for her husband.

"Steve," she said as they started to look around. "I'm exhausted. Can you go upstairs and see if there's anything mom might have tucked away that we should go through first?"

Steve, aware of the drama in Clara's life but not able to internalize their toll for himself, nodded and headed upstairs. Clara slumped down, the weight of the world collapsing her onto the sofa. In addition to all of this, she had the creditors to deal with. Clara looked around at the dusty furniture around her. There was probably enough for Clara to be able to keep the house, something she sorely needed if she and Steve were going to start a family of their own. But beyond that? She'd be lucky if this place didn't have to be stripped bare.

"Clara," Steve yelled down excitedly. "I found something. Come up and see." Clara rose slowly and trod up the stairs to find Steve hunched over an old leather trunk. Though she hadn't thought about it in years, Clara immediately recognized the treasure chest of family memories. She knelt down and carefully opened it. The first thing she saw were the silver bracelets and buckle, even more tarnished than she remembered. Her mother had never wanted to polish them; to keep them the way Meigan had worn them. A pain rose in Clara's chest. She wasn't ready to deal with these heirlooms, not today. She lifted them out of the trunk and put them into a nearby box of things she'd sort through later.

Her gaze then landed on the iconic article about the barn fire. She focused on Meigan's confident stare piercing into her eyes, now judging her for the turns her life had taken. She gently picked the photo up, admiring the confident look, the bracelets, the buckle and the tattoo that had been mistaken for soot. As she looked at the tattoo though, her heart stopped. She blinked her eyes and pulled the photo closer. No, she hadn't been mistaken.

"Steve," she gasped. "This tattoo. That's a peace symbol at the end of her arm!"

Steve squinted. "It sure does look like a peace symbol," he said after a moment. "I didn't know they had that in the 1900s."

"They didn't," Clara said, gasping. "Why … why would she have this?"

Over the next few weeks, they were able to close out the estate. They had found some valuables that let them keep the furniture and even a little bit extra to use towards the baby that would soon be on its way. The trunk and family history gave Clara some purpose as her job search hopes dimmed. She was able to trace her grandfather's past back to 1680, but Meigan … she couldn't find anything about her before 1880. No birth records, no family history. Even by 1880s standards this was unusual. Clara continued diligently but the normally acclaimed researcher was starting to have doubts about her inability to find anything.

As she pursued yet another dead end looking through El Paso County records, slumping back in her chair deflated, the image of the peace symbol tattoo again entered her mind. She reflected on Meigan's mythology and how ahead of her time she seemed, with an attitude that seemed to align more to the young women she saw in the present day. Clara was starting to form an absurd opinion that she couldn't shake.

Maybe Meigan wasn't from the 19th century at all.

Chapter 9

Emily stood on the porch, scuffing her Converse sneakers on the wooden planks badly in need of paint. A strand of her long brown hair slipped forward as she sighed and swung the door open to her mother's house. She knew there was no need to knock first and that the door would be unlocked awaiting her arrival. She turned before entering to see her dad's gray Honda Accord pulling away from the curbside. Emily slumped her shoulders as her black long-sleeved T-shirt hung loosely on her body. She trod inside with the familiarity of someone who had done this many times before.

"Mom, I'm here," Clara's 16-year-old daughter called out as she scanned the front rooms for her mother. Her silver bracelet fell slightly up her arm as she reached to push her hair behind one ear. "Hi honey, I'm upstairs. I'll be down in a minute," Clara called out. "Make yourself at home."

Another weekend with mom, she thought. *I sure hope we do something fun this time.* Clara and her father, Steve, had been divorced for four years now. They had had Emily in 1988, when Clara was in her early forties. Emily glanced outside the kitchen window to the backyard, and a distant memory of a birthday party with the neighborhood kids almost brought a smile to her face. The first few years were a happy childhood, but Clara had started to become obsessed with genealogy and the search for her past.

Emily threw her duffel bag on the sofa and plopped down beside it. Her dark denim skirt shifted as she sank into the cushions, revealing more of the dark opaque tights underneath. She wished she didn't feel like a visitor in her mother's life. Her mind started to wander towards less pleasant memories, like the times her father had to take off work early because

Clara had forgotten to pick her up from school. Looking around, she saw her mother had the spelling bee trophy she had earned in fourth grade on a side table. First place: Edison Elementary. *Nice you keep the trophy out*, Emily thought as she looked at the dusty statue. *Too bad you missed the actual spelling bee.*

The courts had sided with Steve when he said he and Emily needed more time and attention and had given him primary custody. The weekends were the time that Emily had with her mother, and they followed a similar pattern. "What are you doing mom?" Emily asked as she pulled a box of cereal out of the pantry. She knew what the answer was going to be.

"Oh, just working on some genealogy," Clara called down. "I think I may have found some new information about your great-grandmother, Meigan." *Again with Meigan.* "Oh great," she called back to her mom in a feigned voice. "I hope this is the clue that lets you unlock this family mystery."

The Rice Krispies flowed into the bowl and the milk gave them the requisite snap, crackle, and pop.

"Well, we'll see dear," Clara called down. "I found some notes from great-grandpa Evan's mother from 1874. If she knew Meigan then, I'm sure she would have noted something."

"I thought you said you don't have any records before 1880," Emily called back, her mouth half full of cereal. Despite the detachment between them, Emily knew enough of her mother's work to know the theme she was tracking. Her grandmother, Meigan, was a hero who had saved a family from a burning barn in a time when women were not even supposed to talk unless spoken to. In a time before women were expected to have a proper education, she had taught half the girls in town how to read and write before becoming a teacher herself. She was a pioneer woman who juggled a career and a family before women were supposed to have lives outside of the kitchen. There were records of other deeds, but for some reason there was no record of Meigan from before 1880. There was no birth certificate, and no mention of any family lineage. It was as if she had just appeared one day.

"Well, no, I don't. But the more I can show there are no records, the more people will believe me. You know the peace symbol…," Clara started.

"Mom, I told you the peace symbol isn't proof," Emily shouted. "You know that could just be a smudge. Or it could just be a coincidence. I mean, it's not a complex design. It's not impossible to imagine someone drawing a circle with some lines in them back then."

She'd had this argument dozens of times before. Emily focused on her nearly empty bowl of cereal. "Enough dead ends," she muttered. "Just come spend some time with me."

Two hours later, Clara came downstairs to give her daughter a hug. Emily obliged with the physical connection, though it wasn't genuinely felt.

"Good to see you, Emily," Clara said.

"Yeah, same with you mom," Emily replied.

◈ ◈

That evening, Emily was lying on the couch as Clara continued her research upstairs. She rose when she heard a horn honk. Looking outside, she saw a faded blue Buick and a woman with a familiar head of short curly black hair mouthing at her to come outside. "Bye mom," Emily called up to Clara as she grabbed her faded, oversized army jacket. "I won't be out too late." "Have fun, dear," Clara called back down, not bothering to check who Emily was leaving with. Emily hesitated, almost calling back up to let her know where she'd be going, but she knew it would be pointless.

"Nice house," the driver said as Emily entered. "How long have you lived here?"

"I don't live here, Lila," Emily said as she settled into her seat, her eyes looking straight ahead and not at the driver addressing her. "This is my mom's house. I only come here on weekends."

"Oh," Lila said, pausing awkwardly from this response. They pulled out from the curb in silence. A few minutes later Lila attempted to restart the conversation. "Hey, I'm glad you're coming with me to see the show," she said. "No one else was able to make it and I hate driving out of town on my own."

"Yeah, I'm looking forward to it too," Emily said in an emotionless tone of voice, gripping the vinyl seats slightly. "I don't know why no one else from the astronomy club couldn't make it."

"Is your mom OK with you coming if she only sees you on the weekend?" Lila asked gently.

Emily turned to Lila at this question, not sure if she was asking out of concern or curiosity. *Of course she doesn't care*, Emily thought, *I'm not even sure that she knows*. Part of her wanted to believe it was concern and open up to tell Lila more about her mother. She took a deep breath to gather her thoughts before she simply said, "No, she's cool."

They turned onto US-24 and drove towards the mountains. The radio was starting to crackle as they left the city and the signal weakened. Lila stopped trying to make conversation, beyond some occasional comments about the songs that came on as they tuned the radio, and the two of them sat mostly in silence. Finally, they pulled off the highway and drove a mile in towards a large, empty field. The two of them slipped out of the car and, taking a carefully folded blanket out of the backseat, spread it out on the field before laying down on their backs to stare upwards into the inky night sky.

The night was clear and the air was still as they lay and gazed at the heavens. "Look there," Lila said, pointing towards the sky. "You can see them all lining up. Order in the vast nothingness."

Emily nodded as the rare planetary alignment was taking shape before their eyes. "Yeah. The universe is huge," she said basking in her smallness against the dark, twinkling sky. "Makes you appreciate your real place in it all."

They lay in the field for a few hours before packing their blanket and heading back towards Colorado Springs. The drive back was as silent as their trip out, but this time the silence felt earned.

Chapter 10

The following Tuesday, Emily shuffled into the auditorium with a group of other high school students. Ms. Lovington, their high school drama teacher, was standing on the stage, arguing with the janitor about some water left behind from his cleaning that she worried would interfere with their performance. The janitor, an elder man whose wrinkled face showed that he'd been through his share of productions at this school, simply nodded along with her as she lectured him, showing no signs of whether he was listening or, if he was, whether he cared. As she saw the first group of students arrive, Ms. Lovington turned to greet them.

"Welcome back," she said, opening her arms wide as if preparing to give them a group hug. "The floor's a little slick," she said casting a sideways glance to the janitor who had already started shuffling off towards his next job. "But we should be able to rehearse, nonetheless. Dan, Jason, Susan," she said pointing to three of the children. "Come on up and let's practice your lines from scene 2."

Emily escaped backstage along with a few other kids. Back there, no one expected her to shine. It was a safe place where she could be useful without being seen. She much preferred the hum of the stage lights, making sure the others were their best selves, and the smell of sawdust from the set shop. That's where the performance really happened.

As the cast started their performance, she noticed one of the props was set too far upstage. Knowing it would throw the action off later if no one fixed it, she quietly slipped out to nudge it into place.

After the rehearsal, Emily picked up her backpack and started walking up the aisle to leave for the day. Ms. Lovington called out to her as she was halfway to the auditorium doors.

"Emily," she said, "you did great work back there today." Emily froze for a second and smiled nervously, not sure if the compliment was indeed meant for her. "It's rare to see someone so comfortable with coordinating everything backstage. You should think about directing someday." Emily's pulse quickened at the thought. She mustered a meager, "thank you," before heading out the door.

※ ※

The following year was the last time Emily would see both of her parents together. They were at the Pepper Tree to celebrate Emily's acceptance into UCLA. Her dad had no doubt she'd be accepted given her natural talent and good grades. Still, Emily had read the decision letter three times, hunting for some mistake or clarification, before accepting. Emily was surprised but grateful that Clara had agreed to join them to celebrate. Clara had even arrived on time, dressed in a simple beige skirt with a matching top. She had allowed the hostess to check her coat for her but insisted on wearing the pillbox hat atop her short, curled hair to the table.

Emily was slightly slouched, one elbow on the table as she sat picking at the rice pilaf on her plate, pushing it through the butter sauce to pick up some of the flavor. "Emily, your mom and I are so proud of you," Steve said, attempting to break the silence. "You worked hard for this, and you deserve it," he added. "UCLA is going to be a great place for you to get out and meet people. It will do you good to socialize more, and it will help your career."

Emily didn't respond but shifted a bit uncomfortably in her seat. "Steve, don't pressure her," Clara muttered in her ex-husband's direction. "Let her find her footing in her own time."

"It's OK mom," Emily said still looking down at her plate. "He's right, it will be a good opportunity." The truth was, however, that she had mainly picked UCLA to escape the cold Colorado winters. Being a thousand miles away was also a definite plus.

Chapter 11

The first quarter's class load was heavy. Emily's counselor had advised she start slowly with a balance of three classes, but Emily felt she could tackle a fourth. The course load felt like something she could handle; Calculus 1, Psychology 101, Econ 1, and a General Education Arts class. But Emily hadn't factored in the emotional toll the class sizes would have on her. All but her arts class had over 300 students, packed into an auditorium. It was a distraction that Emily felt distanced her from the instruction and made her question the value of a college education.

At least her arts class was a more reasonable 40 students. She looked forward to escaping the cold lecture halls and entering Dodd Hall on Tuesday and Thursday afternoons, knowing that the crowd she'd be joining in the classroom was still navigable. Even though she sat in the back row and tried not to draw attention to herself at first, the instructor addressed her by name. Gradually, she started contributing to class without being called on and even started to awkwardly reminisce about her other classes with students in the same situation.

As part of an assignment, the class attended a performance of *The Shape of Things* at the Little Theater. Emily paused as she stepped inside, struck by the steep rows of seats and intimate shape of the room. It felt nothing like her high school stage, yet something about it filled her with a warm, familiar calmness. She sat captivated, watching the actors portraying the way people reshaped themselves to be acceptable. She was especially drawn to a later scene between two characters, Adam and Evelyn, alone onstage with the air hanging tight between them. Adam was struggling to explain himself, while Evelyn listened with a stillness that felt dangerous, her silence adding more to the scene than any spoken dialog could. While the scene was emotionally powerful, Emily noticed that the actor playing Adam was stepping slightly out of pace with his words. The impact still landed, but she couldn't help but think a little tightening on the pacing would make the scene that much more powerful.

The following day, Emily shared her thoughts as part of the group discussion in class. Other students nodded along in knowing conformity, not willing to admit that she had picked up on a detail that they had failed to see. Her professor lifted his head half an inch as she spoke, not willing to interrupt the classroom discussion but taking note of this surprising insight.

"Emily," he said as the class ended and students were starting to pack up their bags. "That was some good perspective from you."

"Thanks," Emily said, not quite sure why the professor was sharing this with her.

"You know, this might be a little unorthodox, but I understand there's an opening for an assistant director for one of next quarter's theater performances. It's a small production but they need someone. You might want to look into it."

Emily tugged uncomfortably at her ear. "Oh … no, I don't think I could," she said. "I'm still in my first year."

"True," the professor said, "usually those roles go to older students, but I know you did backstage work in high school and you definitely see something even the upperclassmen miss." After a slight pause he added, "I'm going to go down to talk with the head of the production crew and put in a word for you, I'm sure I can get you in."

Emily stood speechless. She wanted to protest, and opened her mouth halfway, but was unable to muster the words. Her professor hadn't noticed and had already turned back towards his desk to prepare for the next class. "See you next week Emily," he said before she could utter a defense.

❧ ☙

Emily was given the opportunity to assist in a school performance of *Rabbit Hole* the following quarter. She was quietly excited, but nervous at the same time. Most of the cast were two or three years older than her and had years of experience underneath their belts. At that afternoon's rehearsal, the student director had a conflict, and Emily was left to direct alone. She sat, leaning back in a chair in the front row, as her arms flopped onto the armrests beside her.

"Take it from the top," she said as one of the actresses flubbed her opening line. *I don't know if I'll ever pull this off,* she thought. She remembered earlier that day when she had gotten back her economics midterm. C-, circled in red on the top. She'd stared at the red ink so long the lines blurred. *They'll realize for sure I don't belong here.*

Emily glanced up to see the actress playing Becca almost shouting her lines at the one playing Izzy. She snapped out of her spiral and forced herself back into the directing role. "Let's try this again," she said softly. "Remember this is the scene where we're discussing Izzy's pregnancy. There's a lot to go on. You're inches from each other but you also love each other. That's why this hurts. Don't play the anger. Play the disappointment."

The actresses nodded, resetting. Their movements became sharper but truer, their voices trembling with the raw mix of emotions the scene demanded. Emily rose, standing outside the stage, and started pacing slowly to coax the emotional rhythm into place. By the time the scene had reached its breaking point, the air felt changed. The actresses weren't performing anymore; they were living it. Emily let the silence hang after they finished. She smiled, small but certain. She almost didn't speak, afraid that she would ruin the moment. "That," she said softly, "was honest."

Chapter 12

A taxi tore through the streets in Colorado Springs, jolting Emily with every turn. She sat in the back, gripping tightly to the door handle to avoid being knocked off her seat. As the car drove down a residential road, she looked knowingly outside. *My old neighborhood*, Emily thought as the car drove past familiar houses. *I haven't been here in eight ... no, nine years.* The car sped past her mother's house, the porch just visible long enough for Emily to catch the sight of a pile of newspapers left out in the cold as they sped past. *No time to stop by the house now*, she thought. *I have to get to the hospital.*

Emily had moved away for college and never came back. There was no reason to. Her father had remarried and moved to Pittsburg, and her mom. Well, her mom had continued in her obsessive behaviors. She had become more and more of a hermit over the years. When Emily did call her mother on major holidays out of a sense of obligation, it always felt like she was interrupting something in Clara's life.

The doctors weren't even sure how long the cancer had been in her system. Would the situation have been different if she hadn't stopped attending church two years ago? If she still had been going to her book club? If she had someone to confide in with how she was feeling, or how the disfiguring lumps had been forming?

Despite their distance, Emily couldn't help but tear up as she entered her mother's room. She wasn't conscious, but unlike many people in this situation she didn't look peaceful. She looked ... incomplete. Emily knew that her life's quest to find connection with her past and her grandmother was about to reach its final dead end.

Emily's phone buzzed to indicate an incoming text message. It was Carl. Emily put the phone down; she certainly didn't have time to think about this now. Even if there were she wouldn't know how to answer. Ever since her microdrama about a girl whose selfie changed while her real face stayed fixed had gone viral, producers had been wanting to connect with her. *Why me*, she had thought when he first contacted her. *I'm not a director. I just got lucky with a Dorian Gray retelling that people liked. I'm nothing special.*

As she sat there with those thoughts, she almost didn't notice that the monitors watching over her mother were starting to beep more rapidly. She was pushed aside as nurses raced into the room, frantically checking vital statistics and calling out for other staff to assist.

❧ ☙

Emily fumbled with the keys as she stood on the front porch after the funeral. *It was a lovely service*, she thought to herself as she stepped over the pile of newspapers. She knelt down to pick up that morning's paper, the only one not stiff and swollen from days in the cold. The priest had said a nice eulogy about Clara's time helping the church arrange their genealogy records. It was too bad that Clara had focused so much on the past and not on the family in front of her. Emily was able to say a few words, but not being asked to give the eulogy stung.

Emily went to the kitchen table to make herself some tea to calm her jitters. Out of habit, she opened the cabinet drawer. She was shocked to find a lone box of Rice Krispies. Tears in her eyes, she picked up the box and looked at the bottom to read EXPIRATION DATE OCTOBER 2007. She froze enough to hear her own heartbeat. Her mother must have bought this box just after she had left for college. *Mom kept this hoping I'd come back*, she thought as she put the box of cereal back.

She sat down at the kitchen table, a swirl of emotions washing over her. *I need something to take my mind off things*, she thought as she unrolled the newspaper in her hand. *I wonder if they still run Garfield*. Emily started flipping through the pages looking for the comics when she passed the local interest section. She stopped for a moment looking at some pictures accompanying a story about old western trends. She saw a picture of a teenage girl with long flowing hair, nose piercing, silver bracelets, and a tattoo proudly showing off a shiny new belt buckle. *Kind of looks like great-grandma Meigan*, she thought before flipping to the comics section on the next page.

After finishing the comics, Emily decided it was time to start sorting through her mother's belongings. In the study, she found boxes of notes and trinkets from the family tree. Arcs of the story headed back to the late 1600s, but most of it was centered about her great-grandmother, Meigan.

"Ah Meigan," Emily said sarcastically, "haven't heard about you before."

Emily opened a box marked "Meigan's pictures." She shifted through it and saw sitting right on top the photograph that her mother had shared with her so many times before. *There she is in all her glory*, she thought. *The pinnacle of courage and virtue that I could never be in my mom's eyes.* The picture, faded slightly with the passage of time, still showed a proud, confident frontier woman in the aftermath of a barn fire. The woman in the picture stared back quietly, as if she saw something in her that Emily had never managed to see in herself.

Emily squinted at the photo more closely, and specifically at the exposed arm. As she examined it more closely, she began to doubt whether it was a peace symbol at all. She knew from her work in theater that it wasn't hard to manipulate photographs even in the early 20th century. Even if it wasn't intentional, the lighting and angles weren't the most optimal when that picture was taken. It could very well just be some soot, or even a tattoo that just resembled a peace symbol when looked at just the right way.

She did really look good in that buckle though, Emily thought, looking at the buckle around her great grandmother's waist.

Emily opened another box marked "Silver trinkets." *This could be good*, she thought, not sure if there would be more sentimental or valuable items inside. She started taking out a few different items, some silverware from her mother's wedding, a tarnished silver tray that may have been used by her grandmother. And towards the bottom of the box ... the iconic buckle.

"Ah," she said picking up the buckle and then looking back at the photo. "Yep, this is the same buckle. Tarnished, but I can see the design work on the front is a perfect match." She held the buckle in her hands, feeling its weight and the connection to history and her own lineage.

She turned the belt buckle over in her hands and stopped cold, dropping the buckle to the floor. There on the back she had seen the inscription, weathered with age but perfectly readable.

MADE IN CHINA

The words processed through Emily's mind. Meigan's belt buckle, the one that had been handed down through generations, wasn't from the 1880s. It was a modern-day artifact. It proved what her mother had suspected – that Meigan was in fact from modern times. Emily darted back to the open newspaper on the kitchen table. That picture in the morning paper? It wasn't just someone that looked like her great-grandmother ... IT WAS HER!

Emily tilted her chair back, almost knocking over a fern in the corner. She didn't notice. Her head was a whirl of thoughts and emotions. Could she approach the family legend and speak with her today? Could she absorb some of her mythos? As these thoughts came together, she didn't even notice that she was already out the door with the morning paper and the photo from 1908 clutched in her hands.

She wandered in a daze down the street for twenty minutes, only half aware of her surroundings. She didn't even notice when she bumped into someone walking towards her, a young boy wearing a jacket with faded constellations stitched into the front.

"Oh, sorry Ryan," Emily said after the impact, recognizing one of the younger colleagues from her astronomy club. "I didn't see you." Ryan was a nice kid. A reflective type, she had enjoyed talking with him despite the fact he was still in high school.

"Oh, hi Emily," Ryan replied dryly. Then, noticing her newspaper, he added nonchalantly, "that was a nice piece about old western wear, wasn't it? I just saw that girl," he added, pointing to the photo accompanying the article. "Nice girl, though a little lost."

"Wait, what?" Emily's mind raced. "You just saw her? Are you sure? Where?"

Ryan could sense Emily's excitement. "Yeah, just five minutes ago," then spotting the older 1908 photo clutched in her hand he noted, "huh, looks like it runs in the family. She has the same pose and belt buckle. Is that her mom?"

"Where is she, Ryan? Please, I have to see her."

"Whoa, whoa, Emily. She was at Loyal Coffee, just down on Nevada Street. She might still be there."

"Thanks Ryan," Emily said, breaking out of her daze and starting in a sprint towards the coffee house. "You have no idea what this means to me!"

As she turned the corner on Nevada Street, she saw Meigan already out of the coffee shop and heading in the opposite direction. Though she couldn't see her face and she had a younger form, the resemblance to the long-treasured family photo was remarkable. Surely this must be the same woman that had dominated the family's mythos for generations.

"Meigan!" Emily shouted out, her voice drowned by the hustle and bustle of the busy street as she ran closer. "Meigan!"

Meigan stopped and turned around, just for an instant. She didn't see Emily but looked in her direction long enough for Emily to see her eyes. And with that glance Emily froze. She didn't wave or shout back, because what she saw wasn't the look of confidence. It was a look of confusion, of insecurity, of fear. In those eyes Emily saw the same traits she saw in herself, and it was jarring.

Is this Meigan? she thought. *The same woman who fought for women's literacy decades before it was a thing? Who made headlines for saving a boy from a devastating fire?*

For a moment Emily wasn't sure. But she saw the buckle. The silver bracelets. And the tattoo. Yes, this was definitely her. Emily couldn't speak and, in a moment, Meigan turned back around. She took another step … and vanished. City life continued as if she had never existed. No one had seen her go. No one but Emily.

That night, Emily stood alone at her mother's house, a half-full glass of Merlot swishing in her hand. She was still trying to make sense of the day's events. She raised the glass to take a sip, then walked over and drew the shades on the window, opening it a crack to let the cool spring breeze in. She stood there, breathing in the fresh dewy air. Placing the glass on the windowsill, she spread the objects that remained of Meigan on the table. The newspaper articles both from a hundred years ago and just that morning laid side by side. The bracelets sat silently beside the buckle. They no longer felt like evidence. They felt like they were residue.

Emily picked up the buckle again, turning it over to trace the worn letters with her thumb. MADE IN CHINA. As she reflected, she noticed the tall, slender curio cabinet in the corner. Among the artifacts covered in dust, one stood out to her, the spelling bee trophy she had won in elementary school. She stared, her face blank as she remembered the tournament her mother had missed and her winning word, "dynasty." She smiled as she thought not about being forgotten, but about her mother's life-long obsession and how this encounter would have put it to rest. And with that, something inside her loosened.

Mom had misunderstood Meigan, Emily realized, as the pain from her mother's absence rose from her chest. She drew in a steady breath as she picked up her phone and scrolled through the text messages, finding the one from Carl from a few days ago. She read it and with nimble fingers typed out a response: *Love the direction you're thinking with the Victorian period piece, this is definitely in my wheelhouse. Let's meet next week.*

With that, she stacked the articles, leaving the buckle to the side as she turned out the lights. Tomorrow felt suddenly, quietly possible.

Thank you for spending time with this story. It began with the premise of a woman stepping into another time and the narrative eventually meeting the moment she vanished. The generations that followed emerged as the echo deepened.

If it stayed with you in any way, I'm grateful for however you choose to share it.

Made in the USA
Coppell, TX
31 January 2026